the
Little
MERMaiD

For my own Mermaid.
I.B.

THE LITTLE MERMAID
A PICTURE CORGI BOOK 978 0 552 55226 4 (from January 2007)
0 552 55226 7

First published in Great Britain by Doubleday,
an imprint of Random House Children's Books

Doubleday edition published 2005
Picture Corgi edition published 2006

1 3 5 7 9 10 8 6 4 2

Picture Corgi Books are published by Random House Children's Books,
61–63 Uxbridge Road, London W5 5SA,
a division of The Random House Group Ltd,
in Australia by Random House Australia (Pty) Ltd,
20 Alfred Street, Milsons Point, Sydney, NSW 2061, Australia,
in New Zealand by Random House New Zealand Ltd,
18 Poland Road, Glenfield, Auckland 10, New Zealand,
and in South Africa by Random House (Pty) Ltd,
Isle of Houghton, Corner Boundary Road & Carse O'Gowrie,
Houghton 2198, South Africa

THE RANDOM HOUSE GROUP Limited Reg. No. 954009
www.kidsatrandomhouse.co.uk

A CIP catalogue record for this book is available from the British Library.

Printed in China

the *Little* *MERMaiD*

Adapted from *the* original by
Hans Christian Andersen

by Ian Beck

PICTURE CORGI

Once, long ago, out where the ocean was at its deepest, and where the sea was as blue as crystal, there lived a great sea king. The king had six daughters, each a beautiful young mermaid. But the most beautiful of all was the king's youngest daughter. Her skin was as pale as the palest rose petals and her eyes were the colour of the ocean itself.

The youngest mermaid loved to hear the king's stories about the strange and distant world of humans above the sea. A world where people walked on legs. A world where you could smell the perfume of the flowers, and where the wind blew with a sigh through tall green trees.

When the little mermaid reached her fifteenth birthday, she was allowed to swim up to see the strange human world for herself. She swam all the way up to the surface of the sea.

For the very first time she was able to sit on a rock above the waves and brush out her long hair in the warm wind.

Just then, she saw a sailing ship anchored nearby. The little mermaid hid herself in the curls and billows of sea foam and swam over to take a closer look at it. Through the glass portholes she could see that the humans were having a party. A handsome young man was celebrating his birthday.

The little mermaid watched, enchanted, as rockets and fireworks were fired from the ship, lighting up the night sky with their bright, colourful stars. The crew sang to the young man, whom they called Prince Caspar. The little mermaid fell in love with him at once.

As the party came to an end, the little mermaid felt a change in the movement of the waves. A storm blew up. The waves swelled, and a great wind tore the sails and smashed the masts of the ship.

The poor sailors were scattered across the crashing waves, and she saw Prince Caspar fall through the stormy sea down towards her home, the kingdom under the waves. The little mermaid knew that humans could not live under the ocean and that the handsome prince would soon drown. She plunged after him and kissed him on the mouth, filling his lungs with air. His eyes opened for a brief moment, and Prince Caspar looked back into the loving eyes of the little mermaid.

The little mermaid swam with easy strength and pulled the prince to safety on a sheltered sandy beach. Then she swam a little way off from the shore and hid herself among the tendrils of seaweed and foam. She watched over the prince as he slept on the sand.

Then the sun rose and still the little mermaid watched anxiously as the prince woke and stretched, looking all about him in bewilderment. Then some humans came from a palace on the cliffs and she saw them tend to the prince. When she was quite sure that he was safe, she dived below the waves and returned to her home in the depths.

The little mermaid dreamed of Prince Caspar and the bright world above the waves. She longed to see the blue sky and feel the wind in her hair, and she longed to see the prince again. While she tended her father's garden, or when she was playing with her sisters, she could think of nothing but the world above the water and the man she had fallen in love with.

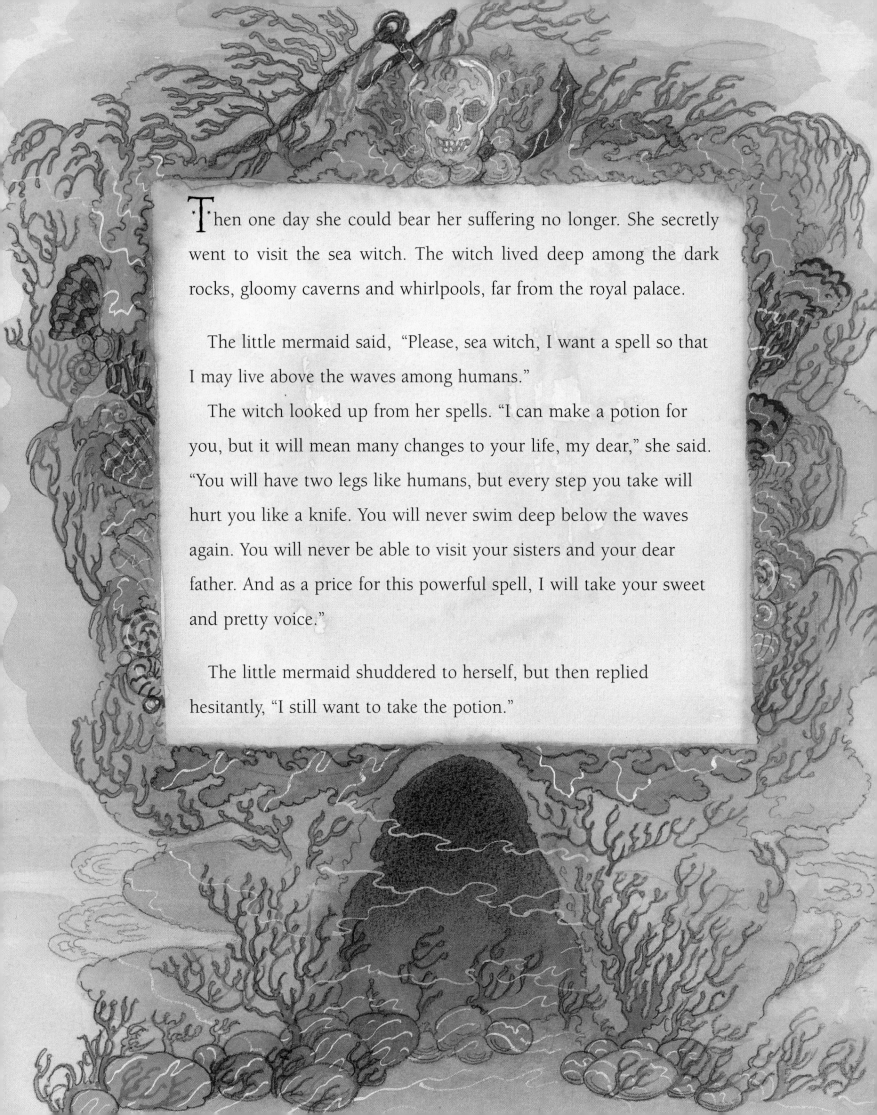

Then one day she could bear her suffering no longer. She secretly went to visit the sea witch. The witch lived deep among the dark rocks, gloomy caverns and whirlpools, far from the royal palace.

The little mermaid said, "Please, sea witch, I want a spell so that I may live above the waves among humans."

The witch looked up from her spells. "I can make a potion for you, but it will mean many changes to your life, my dear," she said. "You will have two legs like humans, but every step you take will hurt you like a knife. You will never swim deep below the waves again. You will never be able to visit your sisters and your dear father. And as a price for this powerful spell, I will take your sweet and pretty voice."

The little mermaid shuddered to herself, but then replied hesitantly, "I still want to take the potion."

So, filled with great sorrow, the little mermaid secretly slipped away from her father and her sisters. She took the hidden shell full of potion from the sea witch, and drank it back in one draught. And as she floated up to the surface of the sea, she felt a strange feeling in her body.

When the little mermaid broke through the waves she gasped for air, and as she swam on the surface she realized how weak she was now. Her new legs were no substitute for the strength of her mermaid's tail. She allowed herself to drift in with the waves, up onto the beach.

Then she stood for the first time and walked. It was just as the witch had predicted: each step hurt her like a knife. She looked back at the peaceful blue sea and the cheerful white waves, and was filled with sadness at the thought that she would never be able to go down to her happy home again.

The little mermaid walked across the beach below the cliffs and the palace. Just then, two young girls ran over to her.

"Have you been in a shipwreck? Where are your clothes?" they asked.

The little mermaid tried to speak but could make no words. The witch, after all, had taken her voice. She shook her head and pointed at her mouth.

"She can't speak," said one girl. "Poor girl, we must take her to the palace to feed her and get her dressed."

At the palace the little mermaid was dressed in fine silks. Her hair was brushed by the court hairdresser, her skin glowed, and her lips were tinted the clear red of a poppy. She looked more beautiful than ever.

In the evening she was introduced to the prince. He was struck at once by her beauty, and also something about her seemed familiar to him. She was like someone he had seen before, but only in a dream. He called her his "little foundling girl".

The little mermaid stayed at the palace and became very close to the prince. They would walk together on the beach, and the little mermaid would gaze out to sea, remembering her father and her sisters. She was so happy to be with the prince, but she missed her life below the waves. Sometimes in the evening she would sit alone on the rocks at the shoreline, and her sisters would come and swim round the rocks and tell her how much they and their father missed her.

One day in the palace garden, the prince took the little mermaid's hand, looked into her eyes, and said, "Little foundling girl, you know that I love you. I think that I have since the moment I first saw you. Yours was the face I saw when I was shipwrecked and drowning, and dreamed that I was rescued by a mermaid."

The little mermaid smiled up at him.

"My father says that I must marry…" the prince said.

The little mermaid squeezed his hand. At last, she thought, he has remembered me.

"… which means I shall be leaving here. I must visit a far-off kingdom where the princess I am to marry lives. I have been very happy here with you and the sea for company, but I have a duty to marry well. It will cement two great nations in peace."

The little mermaid let go of his hand. She held back her tears. The prince kissed her forehead, took her hand, and they continued their walk among the scented flowers.

"I knew you would understand," said the prince.

The whole court travelled together in the royal ship.
The king, his courtiers, the prince, footmen, cooks
and, of course, the beautiful little foundling girl.

As they crossed the ocean, the little mermaid's
sisters swam in the crests of the waves. She sat
secretly on the deck at night and they talked to
her. Her sisters knew how unhappy she was,
and promised to help if they could.
They said they would visit the old sea
witch and ask her what could be done.

The next night, when her sisters returned, the little mermaid
saw that there was something strange about them. They had
cut off all their beautiful hair.

"We sold our hair to the sea witch, and she gave us this
special dagger. If you take it into the prince's chamber on his
wedding night and kill his bride as she sleeps, you will be the
one that the prince loves and you will be happy for ever!"

Her sisters plunged under the sea, leaving the little
mermaid holding the gleaming dagger.

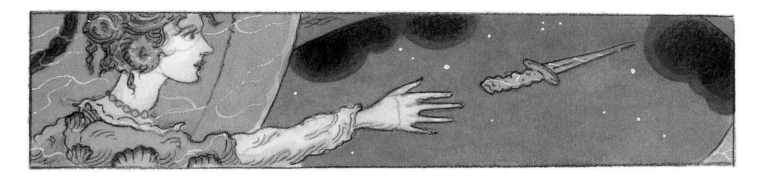

At last the day of the wedding came. The prince married his beautiful princess bride. As the little mermaid watched fireworks shooting into the starlit sky, she remembered the first time she had seen Prince Caspar. It seemed a long time ago.

While the ship slept, the little mermaid stole into the chamber of the prince and his bride, who were peacefully asleep. She took the witch's dagger from her robe. Here was the little mermaid's chance for happiness: all she had to do was bring the dagger down hard.

But she stopped. She could not harm the innocent princess for her own selfish happiness.

The little mermaid went quickly to the cabin window and she threw the dagger as hard as she could back into the sea. It fell with a silvery splash beneath the waves. At that moment she renounced her love of the prince for ever. She went back to the bed and kissed him once on the forehead.

The little mermaid left the chamber and went up onto the deck of the ship. She took off her fine robes and stood on her painful human legs on the side rail of the ship. Next, she plunged into the white foam of the sea.

The little mermaid expected to drown as a human would, to dissolve into the foam and be lost for ever. But when her body entered the water she felt a sudden sensation of strength as her tail returned to her. She was a little mermaid once more!

She dived down into the dark waters and saw her beloved sisters, who were waiting for her. They told her that the sea witch's spell had dissolved the moment the little mermaid had thrown away the dagger.

The little mermaid was soon reunited with her kind father in his beautiful sea palace. Here was where she could be truly happy.

Sometimes at night the little mermaid would swim up to the surface and sit on the rocks, brushing her hair and looking across at the warm lights of the palace. She hoped that the prince would remember fondly his little foundling girl.